Leprechaun Cake and Other Tales

A Vegetarian Story-Cookbook

This book is dedicated to my children:
Tim, Phil & Melissa,
for indulging a mother who still believes in
leprechauns in the woods, trolls beneath bridges,
dragons in Loch Raven & the unicorn up the road.
VWC

Since earning a Bachelor of Science in Art/Education from Towson State University, Vonnie Winslow Crist has illustrated a number of books including *Simple, Lowfat & Vegetarian, Lean & Luscious, More Lean & Luscious, Oat Cuisine, Lean & Luscious & Meatless, The Meatless Gourmet, Hungry Ghosts*, and *How Djambawa Found What He Was Seeking* (unpublished). Her illustrations appear regularly in *Vegetarian Journal, Lite Magazine*, and *Late Knocking*. Vonnie's fiction has won awards in the following competitions: 1993 Lite Circle Fiction Contest; Maryland State National League of American Pen Women Fiction Competition (1993, 1991, 1989); 1993 Black Hills (South Dakota) National Children's Fiction Contest; and 1992 Helen Fries Trigg National Fiction Contest.

Books By Debra Wasserman:

Simply Vegan - (With Reed Mangels, Ph.D., R.D.)

Meatless Meals For Working People - (With Charles Stahler)

No Cholesterol Passover Recipes - (With Charles Stahler)

The Lowfat Jewish Vegetarian Cookbook

Leprechaun Cake and Other Tales

A Vegetarian Story-Cookbook

Stories and Pictures by
Vonnie Winslow Crist

Recipes by
Debra Wasserman

The Vegetarian Resource Group
Baltimore, Maryland
March 1995

✤✤✤ Acknowledgments ✤✤✤

Thank you to Charles Stahler and Debra Wasserman for their support. Thank you also to Tina Buker, Carole Hamlin, Leon S. Josowitz, Reed Mangels, Ph.D., R.D., Israel Mossman, Rosanne Silverman, Elsa Vorwerk, and Marla Wasserman for proofreading the manuscript and Wayne Smeltz for the *Jaguarundi Chili* recipe. Thank you to my sister and brother-in-law, Debbie and Al Bourgeois; my sisters-in-law, Becky and Anne Crist; and my nieces and nephews, Ryan, Jill, Stacy, Paul, and Michael, for their input. Thank you to my mother, Alice Crosby Winslow for being my hand model. And finally, a special thank you to my husband Ernie, who believes in me, even on days when the magic is hard to find.

Project Supervisor -- Charles Stahler
Typeset and Design -- Win-Cri Enterprises

Stories and pictures - Copyright 1995 by Vonnie Winslow Crist

Recipes from: *Meatless Meals for Working People* - Copyright 1986,
1990, 1991, 1994 by Debra Wasserman & Charles Stahler
***No Cholesterol Passover Recipes* - Copyright 1986, 1994**
by Debra Wasserman & Charles Stahler
***Simply Vegan* - Copyright 1991, 1995 by Debra Wasserman**
***The Lowfat Jewish Vegetarian Cookbook* - Copyright 1994**
by Debra Wasserman

Published by The Vegetarian Resource Group
PO Box 1463, Baltimore, Maryland 21203

Library of Congress Cataloging-in-Publication Data
Leprechaun Cake and Other Tales -- A Vegetarian Story-Cookbook/
Vonnie Winslow Crist & Debra Wasserman.
Library of Congress Catalog Card Number: 94-61558

ISBN (Soft-Cover): 0-931411-13-0

Printed in the United States of America
10 9 8 7 6 5 4 3 2 1

✤✤✤✤ Table of Contents ✤✤✤✤

✛✛✛✛✛✛ Foreword ✛✛✛✛✛✛

Since childhood, I have read, collected, and told stories filled with magical creatures. The shelves in my home are lined with well-worn copies of myths, folklore, and fairy tales from many cultures. The mother of two sons and a daughter, I have shared my love of books with them and value the hours we spent reading as a family.

I am also an avid cook. My children and I have delighted in cooking together, especially for holidays and celebrations, since they were very young. As a result of these experiences, I decided to combine modern fantasy tales and nutritious recipes in a book for children and adults to enjoy together.

I approached *The Vegetarian Resource Group* with my proposal for a *Story-Cookbook*, because I have found the recipes published in their cookbooks and their magazine, *Vegetarian Journal*, to be wholesome, delicious, and multi-cultural. Their enthusiastic support of this project has made *Leprechaun Cake and Other Tales - A Vegetarian Story-Cookbook*, a joy to work on.

It is my hope, that *Leprechaun Cake and Other Tales* will be a fun introduction for children, and the adults* who love them, to fantasy literature and healthful cooking.

Vonnie Winslow Crist

*A few suggestions for adults: Work with children, have patience, and make sure you compliment them. Be aware of safety issues, point out where to be careful, and be prepared to help your child. Be ready to discuss recipes that might not turn out "perfect." Try to include the foods you make together in a meal. Most important, make reading and cooking fun family activities.

✥✥✥ Keys to Cooking ✥✥✥

Getting Started

❖ 1) Ask an adult for permission to cook. Tell him or her whether you will need help for some parts of the recipe.

❖ 2) Pick a recipe and check your kitchen for the ingredients. (If you do not have the ingredients for the recipe you selected, make that recipe another day. Choose a different recipe you *do* have the ingredients for to make today.)

❖ 3) Wash your hands and rinse off any fresh vegetables or fruits you will be using. Make sure your work area is clean, too.

❖ 4) Tie back long hair and roll up long sleeves. If you would like to wear an apron, put it on now.

❖ 5) Gather the bowls, spoons, pots, measuring cups and spoons, and ingredients together so you can begin to make the recipe.

❖ 6) If the recipe you have chosen requires baking, ask an adult for help with the oven.

Cooking Terms

Boil: Water or other liquid is heated to 212 degrees Fahrenheit or 100 degrees Centigrade. The liquid will bubble and you may see steam. Be careful of the hot water and steam.

Chopped: A fruit, vegetable, or some other food is cut into small pieces, often with a knife.

Core: The center of an apple or some other food is cut away with a knife or peeler.

Cube: A fruit, vegetable, or some other food is cut into small blocks or cubes.

Drain: The liquid in a can or pot is emptied out into the sink. The food is held in the can or pot by its lid, or use a collander or strainer. If the liquid is hot, be careful of steam.

Finely Chopped: A fruit, vegetable, or some other food is cut into very small pieces with a knife.

Grate: Using a grater, little pieces of a vegetable or spice are shaved off into a bowl or measuring cup. Be careful of your fingers, especially as the vegetable or spice becomes smaller.

Ground: A spice or other food is crushed until it becomes powdery or, in the case of nuts, until they are in very small pieces.

Knead: Bread dough is mixed in a lump by pressing, pulling, and turning with the hands.

Mash: Using a fork or a potato masher to press fruits or vegetables into a soft mixture.

Mix: Using a spoon, ingredients are mixed until they are blended. (Some recipes use the word *stir* which also means *mix*).

<u>Optional</u>: Extra steps or ingredients in a recipe that the cook chooses to use or to not use. You do not have to do these steps.

<u>Peel</u>: Removing the outside peel of a fruit or vegetable with your hands or a peeler. An adult may use a knife.

<u>Pour</u>: To empty the liquid, batter, or other food into another bowl or pot.

<u>Quarter</u>: To cut a food into four equal pieces.

<u>Sauté</u>: To fry or cook food quickly in a small amount of oil or margarine. The cook needs to stir the food occasionally while cooking. Be careful of hot oil or margarine splashing out of the pan. Many cooks today do not use oil, but use water or a vegetable cooking spray.

<u>Simmer</u>: To boil liquid gently, usually over low heat.

<u>Slice</u>: Using a knife, a vegetable or fruit is cut into thin pieces.

<u>Stir</u>: Using a spoon, ingredients are stirred until they are blended. (Some recipes use the word *mix* which also means *stir*).

<u>Stir-fry</u>: To fry or cook food in a small amount of liquid or oil, stirring the whole time.

<u>Variations</u>: Other ways of making the same recipe to change the taste slightly.

Clean-Up Time

☼ 1) Put ingredients back where you found them.

☼ 2) Clean dirty bowls, spoons, pans, and other cooking utensils. Wipe up the area where you prepared the food.

☼ 3) Wash and **dry** your hands. Remember never touch an electrical switch or plug with wet hands or while standing on a wet floor.

☼ 4) Unplug the blender.

☼ 5) Make sure the oven or stove is turned off.

☼ 6) Thank the adult who helped you cook.

☼ 7) Time to eat!

Safety Tips

☞ 1) Have an adult in the kitchen when using a knife. If you do not know how to use a knife, have an adult help you. Remember, a knife is a cooking tool, not a toy!

☞ 2) Always cut away from the body. Never cut with the knife blade pointed towards your body.

☞ 3) Have an adult help with the stove or the oven. Turn pot handles toward the side. Remember to use pot holders or oven mitts when handling hot pots, pans, lids, and dishes.

☞ 4) Turn off the oven or stove when you are finished cooking.

☞ 5) Always have an adult help you if you are boiling water. Water is heavy and it boils at 212 degrees Fahrenheit. Even the steam from boiling water could burn a careless cook.

☞ 6) Do not leave pot holders, mitts, or towels on or near the stove. It may still be hot even though the stove is turned off.

☞ 7) Make sure to tie back long hair, fold up long sleeves, and remove any dangling ties or long ribbons when cooking.

☞ 8) Every kitchen should have a fire extinguisher, and a good cook knows how to use it.

☞ 9) Ask an adult to be in the kitchen when you use a blender. Never put your hands in the blender when it is plugged in. Unplug the blender when you are finished using it.

☞ 10) It is important to wash the fruits and vegetables you use in cooking. Also make sure your hands and work surface are clean. Remember never touch electrical switches or plugs with wet hands or while standing on a wet floor.

☞ 11) If you have younger children in your home, make sure they do not go near the knife, blender, or stove.

☞ 12) A good cook is a safe cook - but accidents still happen. Know first aid procedures for a small cut or a minor burn. Call your doctor if the cut or burn is more serious.

Leprechaun Cake

It was a rainy spring day. The sky was gray, and big raindrops made drum sounds on the roof. Bina was bored.

"Can David come over to our house to play?" she asked her mother.

Bina's mother looked up from the book she was reading. "Yes, Bina, as long as the two of you are quiet. Remember, your brother is taking a nap."

Bina did a happy little dance. She called her next-door neighbor and best friend on the phone. "Hi, David," said Bina.

"Hi, Bina. How are you today?" asked David.

"I'm fine. My mom said you may come over if it is okay with your parents," said Bina.

"I will ask them if it's okay," answered David. He set the phone down and asked his parents if he could visit Bina. "My mom and dad said yes," David told Bina. "I'll come over in a few minutes."

When David came into Bina's kitchen, he was very wet. Bina let David borrow her slippers to wear while they played.

"What do you want to do?" asked David.

"We could bake something," said Bina, "if it's okay with my mother."

David nodded his head. "That is a great idea."

Bina asked her mother if they could bake some · cookies or a cake for supper

"Yes, Bina. Find a recipe for a cake in one of my cookbooks or magazines. Call me when you are ready to put it in the oven," answered Bina's mother, Mrs. Prabhu.

Bina and David began looking in the cookbooks for a cake recipe.

"Pssst," said a small voice.

Bina and David stared at each other.

"Pssst," said the voice again. "Over here."

The children looked over at the kitchen counter. A tiny man was standing on a cookbook.

"Who are you?" asked Bina.

"A leprechaun," answered the little person.

"What do you want?" questioned David.

"To help you bake my favorite cake," said the leprechaun. "It is in this book."

Bina walked to the counter and picked up the cookbook the tiny man had been standing on. She turned the pages until she saw the recipe for *Leprechaun Cake*. "Here it is," she told David. "Let's make it."

The leprechaun hopped on top of the flour canister. "First," he said, "you will need a bowl and a spoon for mixing."

Bina got the bowl and a wooden mixing spoon out of the kitchen cupboards.

"What else do we need?" David asked the little man.

"Measuring spoons and measuring cups of course!" said the leprechaun, as he hopped off of the flour canister and onto the kitchen counter. Before Bina and David

could blink their eyes, the leprechaun jumped off of the counter and up onto the kitchen table.

"My goodness," said Bina, "you sure do move fast for such a tiny person!"

The leprechaun laughed. Bina and David carried the cooking utensils and the cookbook with the recipe to the table. David began to read the list of ingredients for *Leprechaun Cake* to Bina.

After the children had all the ingredients on the table, Bina said, "There are no eggs in this cake."

"There is no milk or sugar in this cake either," said David.

"No," said the leprechaun with a grin. "A cake doesn't need eggs and milk to be delicious!" The little man did a jig on the table top and sang, "No milk, no eggs, you must wait and see: *Leprechaun Cake* is very tasty!"

"I hope you're right," said David in a worried voice.

The children measured flour, softened margarine, baking powder, baking soda, cinnamon, nutmeg, allspice, cloves, water, maple syrup, and vanilla into the mixing bowl. Bina called her mother into the kitchen to help with the oven.

"This smells good," said Mrs. Prabhu as she watched the two friends stir the mixture. Bina and David agreed. They kept looking around the kitchen for the leprechaun, but he had disappeared when Bina's mother came into the room.

"You may carefully use the knife to core and slice the apples," said Mrs. Prabhu. She watched David and Bina

pour half the cake batter into a baking pan that they had lightly oiled so that the cake would not stick. "I'll sit here until the apples are sliced." After the apples were ready, Mrs. Prabhu walked into the living room. "Call me when it's time to put the cake in the oven," she said.

"We will, Mom," said Bina.

As soon as Bina's mother walked out of the kitchen, the leprechaun hopped from behind the trash can and up onto the table. "Time to lay the apples on top of the batter in the baking pan," said the leprechaun.

"Okay," said David. The children laid the apple slices on top of the batter. Then Bina poured the rest of the cake batter into the pan on top of the apples. David and Bina decorated the top of the cake batter with raisins.

"Put it in the oven and bake it, bake it, bake it," sang the leprechaun, as he did a silly jig on the kitchen table.

THE LOWFAT
VEGETARIAN
COOKBOOK

The children laughed. Bina called her mother into the kitchen to put the cake in the oven. Then they set the timer for thirty minutes. "There," said Mrs. Prabhu, "that cake should be ready at dinner time. When the cake is done, we will ice it with some fresh apple butter that I have in the refrigerator."

"Mmmm, that sounds delicious. What else are we having for dinner, Mom?" asked Bina.

Her mother smiled. "I saw a recipe for *Italian Lentil Stew* in my new cookbook. We'll have that stew for supper. Maybe David would like to stay for supper."

"Yes," shouted David. "But I need to ask my mother and father if it's okay with them."

"May I walk over to David's house to ask his parents, too?" said Bina.

Mrs. Prabhu nodded, yes. She was reading her new cookbook. "Let me know how many will be here for dinner," added Bina's mother.

Bina and David put on their jackets and hurried out the kitchen door. The leprechaun leapt from behind the trash can and ran out the door with them. Then with a hop and a skip and a jump he was gone. The sun was shining and it was still raining a little bit. The children could see a rainbow above the treetops.

"Wow," shouted David, "this has been a great day."

"Yes," agreed Bina, "but what about the leprechaun? How is he going to get a piece of cake?"

"You should invite him to dinner, too," said David.

"I do not think he will come," answered Bina. She looked around her backyard. She did not see the little man.

"Come on," said David as he tugged on her jacket. "Let's ask my parents if I may eat dinner at your house tonight." The children went into David's house and asked his mother and father about dinner. Mr. and Mrs. Berg said David could eat at Bina's house as long as he came home right after supper. As the children were walking back to Bina's house, they saw something hiding behind the watering can.

"Is that you, Mr. Leprechaun?" asked David.

"If it is," said Bina, "I would like you to have dinner at my house tonight so you can taste some of your favorite cake. We are having lentil stew."

The leprechaun hopped out from behind the watering can. "Mmmm, lentil stew. I love lentil stew. I'd like to come to dinner if you're sure your mother will not mind."

Bina smiled. "No, my mother won't mind, but she might be a little surprised. We don't often have leprechauns come to dinner."

The leprechaun laughed. He and David and Bina went into Bina's house. Bina's mother did not mind an extra guest, but she *was* surprised to see a leprechaun. At dinner that night, a wonderful time was had by all and the leprechaun promised to visit his new friends again.

❖❖ Bina and David's ❖❖
❖❖ Favorite Recipes ❖❖

Rainy Day Lemonade
(Serves 6)

4 lemons
2 oranges
8 cups water

1) Cut lemons in half and squeeze out the juice. Remove seeds.*
2) Cut oranges into thin slices and remove seeds.*
3) Place lemon juice, orange slices, and water in a large glass jar or pitcher. Stir.
4) Refrigerate at least 3 hours before serving.
5) Stir and serve chilled.

*Ask an adult to be in the kitchen when you use a knife to slice the lemons and oranges. ☺

Leprechaun Cake

(Serves 9)

3 cups whole wheat pastry flour
5 teaspoons margarine
2 teaspoons baking powder
1 teaspoon baking soda
1 teaspoon ground cinnamon
1 teaspoon ground nutmeg
1/2 teaspoon ground allspice
1/4 teaspoon ground cloves
1-1/2 cups water
1/2 cup maple syrup
2 teaspoons vanilla
3 apples - cored, quartered, and sliced*
Raisins (or other dried fruit, chopped*)

1) Preheat oven to 350 degrees Fahrenheit.**
2) Mix all the ingredients together in a large bowl, except apples and raisins. Pour half the batter into a lightly oiled 9" x 12" pan. Lay apple slices on top of batter in the pan. Cover the apple slices with the remaining batter. Decorate with raisins or chopped dried fruit.
3) Bake at 350 degrees Farenheit for 30 minutes. Cool before removing from pan. Cake can be iced with apple butter.

*Ask an adult to be in the kitchen when you use a knife to slice the apples or chop the dried fruit. ☺
**Ask an adult to help with the oven. ☺

Bina's Fruit French Toast

(Serves 2)

1 banana, peeled
4 large strawberries, fresh or frozen
1/3 cup apple juice
1/2 teaspoon ground cinnamon
4 slices whole wheat bread

1) Use a blender to blend together the banana, strawberries, apple juice, and ground cinnamon.* Pour mixture into a bowl.
2) Soak bread in the fruit mixture.
3) Cook on both sides at medium heat on a lightly oiled or non-stick griddle until just beginning to brown.**

Variations: Use other fruit such as pineapple or blueberries instead of the strawberries.

Ask an adult to be in the kitchen when you are using a blender. Remember to unplug the blender when you are finished blending the fruit mixture. ☺
**Ask an adult to help with the griddle. Remember to use pot holders or mitts when handling hot pans.* ☺

North African Pea Dish

(Serves 5)

1 leek
1 small onion, peeled and finely chopped*
2 cups fresh or frozen peas
1 teaspoon oil
1/4 cup water

1) Rinse leek well and chop off bottom roots. Finely chop entire leek (including leaves).*
2) Sauté leek, onions, and peas in water and oil in a small frying pan over medium heat for 5 minutes.** Serve warm.

*Ask an adult to be in the kitchen when you use a knife to chop the leeks and to peel and chop the onion. ☺
**Ask an adult to help with the stove. Remember to use pot holders or mitts when picking up a hot frying pan. ☺

Italian Lentil Stew

(Serves 6)

1 cup lentils, uncooked
1 cup macaroni, uncooked
15-ounce can tomato sauce
8-ounce can tomato paste
1 onion, peeled and chopped*
1 teaspoon Italian seasoning
1 teaspoon garlic powder
4 cups water

1) Place all the ingredients in a large pot. Cover and cook over medium heat until tender (approximately 20 minutes).** Stir occasionally.
2) Serve hot.

*Ask an adult to be in the kitchen when you use a knife to peel and chop the onions. ☺

**Ask an adult to help with the stove. Remember to use pot holders or mitts when picking up the hot pot. ☺

Mrs. Prabhu's Rice Pudding

(Serves 6)

1 cup instant rice
2/3 cup raisins
2 ripe bananas, peeled and mashed
1/2 cup water
1 teaspoon ground cinnamon
1/4 teaspoon ground nutmeg

1) Cook instant rice according to the directions on the package, adding raisins while cooking rice.* Preheat oven to 350 degrees Fahrenheit.*
2) Pour rice and raisins into a blender cup, and add the rest of the ingredients.** Blend together for 1 minute.
3) Pour into a glass loaf-size baking dish that has been sprayed with vegetable cooking spray. Bake for 20 minutes.

*Ask an adult to help with the stove and oven. Remember to use pot holders or mitts when picking up pots or baking dishes. ☺
**Ask an adult to be in the kitchen when you are using a blender. Remember to unplug the blender when you are finished blending the rice pudding. ☺

David's Favorite Baked Falafel
(Serves 6)

4 cups pre-cooked or canned (two 19-ounce cans)
      garbanzo beans (chickpeas), drained
1 teaspoon dill weed powder
1/2 cup fresh parsley, finely chopped*
1 small onion, peeled and finely chopped*
1 teaspoon garlic powder
1 tablespoon baking soda
1 teaspoon cumin
1/8 teaspoon cayenne pepper
2 tablespoons sesame seeds

1) Preheat the oven to 400 degrees Fahrenheit.** Mash chickpeas in a bowl and add the remaining ingredients. Mix well.

2) Divide mixture into 24 one-inch balls. Flatten each ball with your palm and place on a lightly oiled cookie sheet. Bake at 400 degrees Fahrenheit for 35 minutes. Turn the falafel over. Continue cooking another 15 minutes.

3) Serve 4 falafel per person. Falafel can be served on a bed of lettuce with chopped tomatoes and cucumbers.* You can also serve falafel in pita bread. David and Bina love falafel sandwiches!

*Ask an adult to be in the kitchen when you use a knife to chop vegetables. ☺

**Ask an adult to help you with the oven. Remember to use pot holders or mitts when picking up hot cookie sheets. ☺

Turkish Pilaf
(Serves 6)

1-1/2 cups brown rice
4 cups water
1/4 cup raisins or dried prunes, chopped*
1/4 cup dried apricots, chopped*
2 tablespoons sliced almonds
2 tablespoons shelled pistachio nuts
1 teaspoon ground cinnamon

1) Put 4 cups of water in a pot and heat over high heat until boiling.** Add rice. Lower heat until mixture is boiling gently. Cover and cook for 45 minutes.
2) Stir in remaining ingredients and serve warm.

*Ask an adult to be in the kitchen when you use a knife to chop the prunes and dried apricots. ☺
**Ask an adult to help with the stove. Boiling water is very hot and extra care is needed to prevent burns. Remember to use pot holders or mitts when picking up hot lids or pots. ☺

Sweet Rainbow Delight

(Serves 6)

2 apples, finely chopped*
2 carrots, grated*
1/3 cup shredded coconut
2/3 cup raisins
1/2 cup chopped walnuts*

1) Toss all ingredients in a bowl.
2) Chill and serve.

Variation: Add chopped dates instead of raisins.*

*Ask an adult to be in the kitchen when you use a knife and grater
to chop and grate the carrots, apples, walnuts, and dates.* ☺

Magical Moroccan Couscous

(Serves 4)

1 cup orange juice (or other fruit juice)
1/2 cup water
1 cup couscous
1/2 cup water
1/4 cup pitted dates, finely chopped*
1/4 cup raisins
1/4 cup sliced almonds
1 teaspoon ground cinnamon

1) Bring fruit juice and 1/2 cup water to a boil in a small pot.** Remove from heat. Stir in couscous and allow to sit covered for 5 minutes.

2) Meanwhile, in a separate pan, sauté dates, raisins, almonds, and cinnamon in 1/2 cup water for 2 minutes.** Add cooked couscous.

3) Mix well and serve warm.

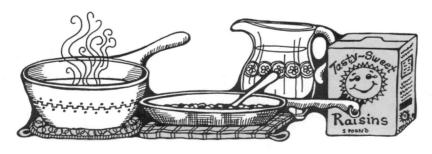

*Ask an adult to be in the kitchen when you use a knife to chop the dates. ☺

**Ask an adult to help you with the stove. Remember to use pot holders or mitts when picking up hot pots and pans. ☺

The Good Luck Dragon

Mitsue lived in the second house from the corner on Park Street with her parents and her Grandma Lee. Grandma Lee used to be friendly with the neighbors. She liked to take walks with Mitsue to the store and to the library. She used to love to work in her flower and vegetable gardens, but not this spring. Mitsue's grandfather had died last fall and now Grandma Lee was quiet and sad. Mitsue told her parents that she was worried about Grandma Lee, but her mother and father said that all Grandma Lee needed was time.

One day while Mitsue was working on her homework, she looked out of her bedroom window and saw a robin building a nest. Mitsue ran into the kitchen shouting, "Grandma, Grandma, come see the robin's nest."

Grandma Lee was making dinner. "Not now, Mitsue. I'm busy. Besides, robins always make nests in that tree."

Mitsue went back to her room. She was worried. Her grandmother usually was the first person in the family to look for bird nests in the spring, but now she did not seem to care.

After several days, Mitsue could see three blue eggs in the nest. She showed the eggs and nest to her parents, but still her grandmother did not come look. One morning when Mitsue looked out of her window, she saw a fourth egg in the nest. It was pink with green spots! Mitsue told her parents and Grandma Lee about the strange egg.

"I have never heard of an egg that color," said her mother. "Perhaps Rosa's brothers are playing a joke."

Mitsue thought about her best friend's brothers, Carlos and Pablo. A trick egg would be a funny joke to them. "You are probably right, Mom," agreed Mitsue.

The next day, the three robin eggs hatched. The pink and green egg did not hatch. When Mitsue told Rosa Sanchez about the strange egg, Rosa asked to see the nest. The girls looked out the bedroom window at the three baby birds being fed, and the pink and green egg that shared the nest with the robins.

"I do not think that egg belongs to my brothers. But don't worry, the mother robin will push that egg out of her nest," said Rosa. "It is too big and her babies need the room."

"But the egg will break and the bird that lives inside it will die," said Mitsue. She felt like crying for the poor pink and green egg's baby bird.

Rosa shrugged her shoulders. "Maybe I'm wrong."

Mitsue knew Rosa was right. When she was getting ready for school on Thursday, Mitsue saw that the pink and green egg was missing. As soon as she ate her breakfast, she hurried outside to find the pink and green egg. She saw it on the ground under the plum tree. It had a small crack in it. Carefully, Mitsue picked up the egg and carried it to her bedroom. She wrapped the egg in an old towel and put it in the sun to keep it warm. Mitsue had to run to catch up with her friend on their walk to school.

"Why are you late this morning, Mitsue?" asked Rosa.

"You were right about that egg. The mother robin did push it out to make room for her babies. I found it on the ground and put it in a warm place in my room," said Mitsue. "You should come and see the egg after school."

"Okay," said Rosa as they arrived at Wood Park Elementary School. Both Mitsue and Rosa were in Mr. Weaver's fifth grade class.

When Rosa and Mitsue walked home from school to the Lees' house, they saw the crack in the pink and green egg had grown larger. "I wonder what kind of bird will hatch out of that egg," said Rosa.

No sooner had those words been spoken, than the egg cracked the rest of the way and out popped a baby dragon. The girls were so surprised that they could not even squeal. The dragon fluttered his green wings and flew up to Mitsue's shoulder.

"Hello, friend," said the baby dragon.

"Hello," said Mitsue with her eyes open wide. "Are you a real dragon?"

"Of course. What else would I be? Now how about some dinner?" answered the dragon.

"What do dragons eat?" asked Rosa, afraid she might not want to know.

"Why," said the dragon, "peas and plums and bread crumbs. We like to eat noodles and nuts and oodles of tofu, too. How about you?"

"I think it's time for me to go home," said Rosa. "*What* are you going to do with that dragon, Mitsue?"

"I'm not sure. I guess the first thing to do is to feed

him," said Mitsue. "Do you have a name, dragon?"

"Lucky," answered the dragon. "I am a good luck dragon."

"Well, good-bye, Mitsue. Good-bye, Lucky," said Rosa as she headed for her house.

"Bye," said Mitsue to Rosa as her friend left. "Lucky, I am not sure my grandmother allows dragons in her house so I'm going to put you in my pocket. I'll drop some food into my pocket while I am at the dinner table. I hope you will find something you like to eat."

"Yum yummy in the tummy. Sounds great to me, says Lucky," sang the dragon.

Mitsue fed Lucky scraps at dinner and breakfast. "Lucky," she told the dragon, "I have two more days of school before summer vacation. You will have to be good until I get home. That means you are not to scare Grandma Lee."

Lucky nodded his small head. "I will be extra good, Mitsue, just for you!" And Lucky was as good as he could be for the next two days. Rosa came over to the house to visit with the dragon both days. The next morning was the beginning of summer vacation. Mitsue slipped Lucky into her pocket and took him with her when she went to play at Bina's house. Mitsue showed Lucky to Bina, David, and the rest of the neighborhood children. All the kids loved the little dragon and brought him peas, plums, bread crumbs, noodles, nuts, and oodles of tofu.

One day when the children were trading baseball cards in Franklin and Tia's basement, David said, "Mitsue,

we never see your grandmother anymore. Is she sick?"

"No," answered Mitsue. "She is still sad because my grandfather died. She doesn't want to visit or take walks or garden like she used to."

"Why not change that?" said Lucky.

"What do you mean?" asked Mitsue. "What can a bunch of kids do to cheer up my grandmother?"

"The Fourth of July Parade is two weeks away, right?" said the dragon. The children nodded their heads. "I have an idea, but all of you will have to work together. Is everyone ready to work on a surprise for the parade?"

All the children said yes, and Lucky told them his plan. Rosa asked Uncle Berto for an old tablecloth that she had seen in the cupboard. Mitsue asked Grandma Lee for needles, thread, buttons, bells, and trim. David asked his parents for some old sheets. Bina asked her mom for the old curtains from her baby brother's room. Kristin asked her dad for the paint and newspapers stored in their shed. Franklin and Tia asked their mother and father to help make flour and water paste for paper mache'. Carlos and Pablo found some balloons they were saving to fill with water and throw at the trash can. They gave the balloons to Mitsue for the surprise. Jasmine asked her mother for some old ribbon. Other children found more sheets, tablecloths, curtains, ribbons, and fabric scraps for the surprise. The children decided to work on the project in Franklin and Tia's basement.

Every day for the next two weeks, the neighborhood children would hurry to Tia and Franklin's basement to

work on the surprise. Soon the neighborhood parents began to ask each other what was going on. No one knew.

Finally the Fourth of July arrived. All the neighborhood children told their parents to make sure to watch the parade. Then the children hurried to Franklin and Tia's house to get ready. Franklin's dad, Mr. Harris, walked the kids to the park where the parade was to begin.

Mr. Harris walked home laughing. He told the neighborhood families to bring their folding chairs over to his front lawn. Bina's mom, David's parents, and the Lee family invited the neighbors to use their front lawns, too, because the parade came down Park Street.

The families watched floats, marching bands, and horses go by. They saw fire engines, old cars, and motor cycles drive by. They laughed at the clowns, cartoon characters, and silly bikes, but they did not see the children.

"Maybe something is wrong," said Mr. Lee.

"Look, there are the kids now," said Mr. Harris.

Then all the neighborhood families saw the surprise the children had been working on. They had made a dragon mask and painted it with bright colors. Then they'd sewn together curtains, tablecloths, sheets, and other pieces of fabric to make a silly dragon's body. The body was decorated with ribbons, buttons, bells, and balloons. All the kids were under the body. As they walked, it looked like the dragon had many legs, each one of them wearing different shoes.

Mr. and Mrs. Harris cheered. Mr. and Mrs. Sanchez and Rosa's Uncle Berto cheered. Mrs. Prabhu and Bina's little brother cheered. David's parents, Mr. and Mrs. Berg, cheered. Kristin's family cheered. Jasmine's parents, Mr. and Mrs. Abdul, cheered. Mr. and Mrs. Lee cheered. Grandma Lee, who remembered the parade dragons from her childhood, cheered the loudest.

When the children's dragon passed by the judge's platform, the crowd laughed and clapped their hands. The judges awarded the silly dragon first prize. The children carried the first prize trophy to Grandma Lee.

"Grandma Lee," said Mitsue as she handed the trophy to her grandmother, "we want you to keep the trophy for the neighborhood."

Mitsue's grandmother was happy to keep the trophy. "Everyone must stop by to see the prize," she said.

"What about now?" said Mr. Lee. "What we need is a neighborhood picnic to celebrate. Everyone is welcome to come to our house for a picnic."

All the neighborhood families brought something good to eat and hurried to the Lees' house for a picnic.

"Your idea worked," said Mitsue to Lucky. "My grandmother is laughing and seeing friends. Many people will visit her to see the prize trophy, too. Thank you."

"You are welcome, my friend," said Lucky with a sigh. "But it's time for me to find another little girl or boy who needs good luck." As soon as he said these words, Lucky, the good luck dragon, fluttered his green wings and flew up above the plum tree.

"Will I ever see you again?" asked Mitsue.

Lucky winked his sparkling green eye and said, "You can never tell when good luck might find you." Mitsue smiled and waved good-bye to Lucky. Then she ran inside to help Grandma Lee with the picnic.

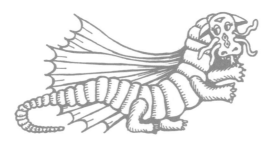

★★★ Fourth of July ★★★ ★★ Picnic Recipes ★★

Quick Fireworks Salsa

(Serves 8)

29-ounce can tomato puree
2 ripe tomatoes, chopped*
1 green pepper - seeds removed, cored and
    chopped*
4 scallions (green onions), chopped*
1/4 teaspoon cayenne pepper**
1 teaspoon garlic powder
Salt to taste (optional)

1) Mix all the ingredients together in a large bowl.
2) Serve with chips.

Variation: Add more cayenne pepper to make salsa hotter!

Ask an adult to be in the kitchen when you use a knife to chop the vegetables. ☺
**If cayenne pepper gets on your hands, wash it off immediately. Cayenne pepper could sting if it gets in your eyes or in a cut. ☺*

Pita Chips

(Serves 8)

3 pita breads
2 teaspoons oil
1 teaspoon paprika
1 teaspoon garlic powder
1 teaspoon crushed oregano
1/2 teaspoon salt (optional)

1) Split pita breads in half. Cut each half into several 2-inch size triangles.*
2) Place the cut bread on a lightly oiled cookie sheet. Sprinkle bread with half the oil, and half the paprika, garlic powder, oregano, and if you prefer, salt.
3) Place the bread under a broiler until it begins to brown (about 3 minutes).** Turn the bread over and sprinkle with remaining oil and spices. Place the bread back under the broiler for 1 minute longer to turn it into chips.
4) Remove the chips. Once the chips are cool they will be crisp and delicious.

*Ask an adult to be in the kitchen when you use a knife to cut the pita bread into triangles. ☺
**Ask an adult to help with the broiler. Remember to use pot holders or mitts when picking up hot pans. ☺

Dragon Party Punch

(Serves 4)

2 cups cranberry juice
2 cups lemonade
1 liter bottle of ginger ale or club soda
1 orange, seeds removed and sliced*
Ice

1) Mix all the ingredients in a large punch bowl.
2) Serve.

Variations: Use different juices or replace orange slices with lemon slices.

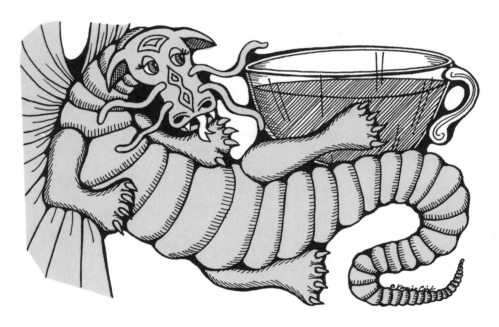

*Ask an adult to be in the kitchen when you use a knife to slice the orange. ☺

Grandma Lee's Fried Rice

(Serves 4)

1 cup basmati rice
2 cups water
2 teaspoons oil
2 stalks celery, finely chopped*
1 large green pepper - seeds removed, cored, and
    finely chopped*
2 scallions (green onions), finely chopped*
1 tablespoon fresh ginger, peeled and grated*
3 tablespoons soy sauce or tamari

1) Cook rice in water until done.** (Follow directions on package).
2) When rice is cooked, add remaining ingredients and stir-fry over medium heat for 5 minutes.
3) Serve.

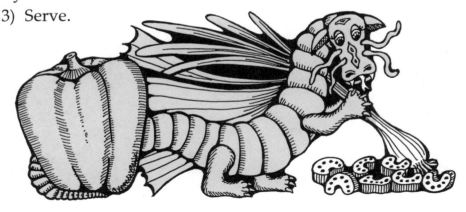

*Ask an adult to be in the kitchen when you use a knife to chop vegetables and a grater to grate ginger. ☺
**Ask an adult to help with the stove. Remember to use pot holders or mitts when picking up hot pans. ☺

Tia's Favorite Applesauce

(Serves 6)

Water
6 apples - cored, peeled, and finely chopped*
    (peels can be left on apples if desired)
1 tablespoon ground cinnamon
1 teaspoon ground nutmeg
2 oranges - peeled, seeds removed, and sliced*

1) Fill the bottom of a large pot with water.
2) Cook apples, cinnamon, nutmeg, and oranges over medium heat, stirring occasionally until the apples are soft.**
3) Remove from heat and serve either hot or cold.

Variation: Add raisins.

Ask an adult to be in the kitchen when you use a knife to chop (and peel) the apples and peel and slice the oranges. ☺
**Ask an adult to help with the stove. Remember to use pot holders or mitts when picking up hot pots.* ☺

Yemenite Bread Salad
(Serves 10)

6 small whole wheat pita breads
    (or 3 large pita breads)
1 pound (about) romaine lettuce,
    torn into bite-size pieces
2 scallions (green onions), finely chopped*
1 cucumber, peeled and chopped into cubes*
2 ripe tomatoes, chopped*
1/2 cup fresh parsley, chopped*
1 tablespoon dried crushed mint
2 tablespoons lemon juice
1/4 cup olive oil
1 chili pepper, finely chopped* (optional)

1) Cut pita bread into bite-size pieces,* place on a pan, and toast in toaster oven or under broiler for a few minutes.**
2) Toss torn lettuce and chopped scallions, cucumber, tomato, parsley, and mint in large bowl.
3) Add lemon juice, olive oil and (if desired) chili pepper. Toss again.
4) Add bread right before serving and toss one more time.

Ask an adult to be in the kitchen when you use a knife to chop vegetables and cut pita bread into pieces. ☺
**Ask an adult to help with the oven or broiler. Remember to use pot holders or mitts when picking up hot pans. ☺*

Israeli Carrot Salad

(Serves 8)

2-1/2 pounds carrots, peeled and grated*
5 temple oranges - peeled, seeds removed and
       chopped*
Juice of one lemon
2 tablespoons crushed dried mint
1 cup raisins

1) Toss all the ingredients together in a large bowl.

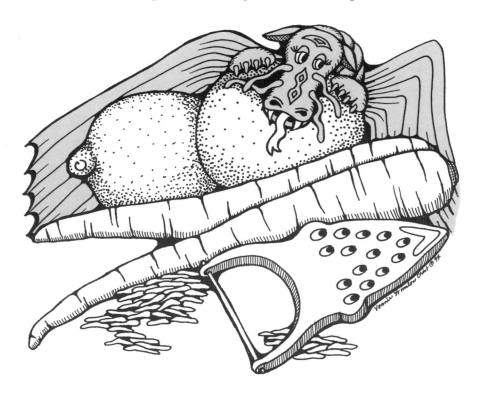

*Ask an adult to be in the kitchen when you use a knife and a
grater to chop, peel, and grate the carrots and oranges.* ☺

Fourth of July
Garbanzo Bean Burgers

(Makes 6 Burgers)

2 cups pre-cooked or canned (two 19-ounce cans) gabanzo beans (chickpeas), drained and mashed

1 stalk celery, finely chopped*

1 carrot, finely chopped*

1/4 cup small onion, peeled and finely chopped*

1/4 cup whole wheat flour

Salt and pepper to taste

2 teaspoons vegetable oil

1) Mix all ingredients except for cooking oil in a bowl.

2) Form 6 flat patties. Fry in oiled pan over medium-high heat until burgers are golden brown.** Turn burgers over and fry on the other side until done.

3) Serve alone or with tomato sauce, ketchup, or barbecue sauce.

Ask an adult to be in the kitchen when you use a knife to chop celery, carrot, and onion. ☺

**Ask an adult to help you with the stove. Remember to use pot holders or mitts when picking up hot pans. ☺*

Lucky's Favorite Romanian Sweet Pasta

(Serves 8)

1 pound eggless pasta
1 cup maple syrup
1/2 cup walnuts, ground, <u>or</u> 1/3 cup poppy
    seeds, ground
1/2 teaspoon lemon rind, finely chopped*
1-1/2 cups raisins
1/2 teaspoon ground cloves
1 teaspoon ground cinnamon

1) Cook pasta according to package directions in 12 cups boiling water until done.** Drain.

2) Heat maple syrup and walnuts or poppy seeds in a large pot over medium-high heat for 2 minutes.** Add lemon rind, raisins, and ground cloves and cinnamon. Continue cooking for 3 more minutes.

3) Add cooked pasta. Mix well and serve warm.

4) You can also pour the mixture into a lightly oiled baking dish and bake at 350 degrees Fahrenheit for 20 minutes before serving.**

*Ask an adult to be in the kitchen when you use a knife to chop the lemon rind. ☺

**Ask an adult to help with the stove and oven. Boiling water is very hot, so be extra careful. Remember to use pot holders or mitts when picking up hot pots or baking dishes. ☺

Pumpkin Casserole

(Serves 5)

29-ounce can unsweetened pumpkin
2 apples - cored, peeled, and chopped*
1 cup raisins
2 teaspoons cinnamon
1/4 teaspoon nutmeg
2 tablespoons molasses
1 cup chopped walnuts*

1) Preheat the oven to 375 degrees Fahrenheit.**
2) Mix all the ingredients together in a bowl. Pour the mixture into a loaf pan that has been sprayed with vegetable cooking spray.
3) Bake at 375 degrees Fahrenheit for 20 minutes.** Serve hot.

*Ask an adult to be in the kitchen when you use a knife and a vegetable peeler to core, peel, and chop the apples and chop the walnuts. ☺

**Ask an adult to help with the oven. Use pot holders or mitts when picking up hot pans. ☺

Vegetable Pancakes
(Serves 2)

2 cups chopped vegetables* (cabbage, scallions or
   green onions, carrots, celery, etc.)
1 cup unbleached white flour
1 cup water
1 tablespoon soy sauce
1 teaspoon ground ginger (optional)
1 tablespoon oil

1) Mix all the ingredients except the oil in a large bowl.
2) Heat oil in a non-stick frying pan over medium heat.**
Form 6 pancakes and fry in oil until lightly browned. Turn
the pancakes over and fry on the other side until done.
3) After frying pancakes, lay them on a paper towel for a
few minutes to drain off excess oil.

*Ask an adult to be in the kitchen when you use a knife to chop
vegetables. ☺
**Ask an adult to help with the stove. Remember to use pot
holders and mitts when picking up hot frying pans. ☺

Yemenite Green Bean Soup

(Serves 6)

1 cup brown rice
2-1/2 cups water
1 pound green beans, chopped*
1 small onion, peeled and finely chopped*
2 teaspoons oil
6 cups tomato juice
2 cups water
Salt and pepper

1) Cook brown rice in 2-1/2 cups water in a covered pot over medium-high heat for 35 minutes.**
2) Meanwhile, sauté green beans and onion in oil in a large pot over medium-high heat for 5 minutes.** Add juice, 2 cups water, and seasonings. Bring to a boil. Reduce heat and simmer over medium heat for 20 minutes.
3) Add cooked rice and simmer 5 minutes longer.** Serve hot.

*Ask an adult to be in the kitchen when you use a knife to chop green beans and onion. ☺
**Ask an adult to help you with the stove. Be extra careful with boiling liquid. Remember to use pot holders or mitts when picking up hot lids and pots. ☺

The Friendship of Deer and Jaguarundi

Each day in September when the neighborhood children came home from school, they liked to go over to the Sanchez family's yard to play soccer. Rosa and her twin brothers, Pablo and Carlos, had a soccer ball. Their Uncle Berto, who lived with the Sanchez family, had made two small soccer goals on either end of the back yard. Uncle Berto stayed at home and watched Rosa, Carlos, and Pablo until their parents returned from work in the evenings. He was a very good cook and prepared most of the meals for their family.

One Friday, as the neighborhood children were trying to play soccer, Pablo and Carlos decided to trick everyone. They kept switching teams and pretending they were both Pablo. It was funny for a few minutes, but soon the other children became angry.

Rosa said to her brothers, "Stop trying to trick everyone. We want to play a game of soccer."

Pablo and Carlos just laughed. "I'm Pablo," they both said. "Carlos is the one starting trouble." Then one of the twins took the ball and ran around the yard with it. He tossed it to his brother. Carlos and Pablo wouldn't let anyone else play with the ball.

All the children began to run after the twins, screaming. Rosa was the most upset of all, because it was her brothers who were causing problems.

"We're going home," said Franklin and his sister Tia.

"Me, too," agreed David.

"What is all of this fighting about?" asked Uncle Berto as he walked out onto the back porch. Uncle Berto was carrying a large jug of ice water and some cups.

"It's Pablo and Carlos. They are playing tricks and ruining our soccer game," said Rosa, with a frown.

"That is right," shouted the children, "and we don't want to play soccer with them anymore."

"Wait a minute," said Uncle Berto. "It's time to take an ice water break and I will tell you a story while you rest. After I tell the story, we'll talk about Pablo and Carlos."

The children each got a cup of water and sat down on the porch. Uncle Berto sat down in his favorite chair and took a drink of water. He smiled at the children and began his tale.

"I will tell you a story from South America about the friendship of Deer and Jaguarundi," said Uncle Berto.

"Once long ago, Jaguarundi and the little forest Deer were friends. Jaguarundi, though only a small, brown jungle cat, was quite brave. The friends would play games together and help each other with their chores. One day Deer would help Jaguarundi sweep his home and the next day, Jaguarundi would help Deer grind flour. Their friendship was strong even though Jaguarundi like to play tricks, because little Deer was pleasant and forgiving.

One day during the warmest part of the summer, Armadillo, dressed in his hard bony shell, came to visit. First he stopped by Deer's wooden home and invited her to Jaguar's wedding feast. Next, Armadillo walked to Jaguarundi's hut with its palm leaf roof and invited him to the wedding. Armadillo visited all of the forest creatures, inviting them to come to the great celebration.

Deer was excited about the upcoming wedding. She worked hard to grind the finest flour. Then she baked a loaf of bread for Jaguar and his bride. Deer also filled a small pot with freshly squeezed fruit juice. She wrapped her gifts in palm leaves and walked to Jaguarundi's house to see if he would like to go with her to the wedding.

Jaguarundi agreed that they should travel together, and so the two friends set out for the celebration. They had not gone far when they came to a stream. Jaguarundi saw a mahogany tree that had fallen across the water. He grinned and leapt onto the slick log with his paws and claws.

"Come across this way, Deer, so you do not get your feet wet," he said.

Deer looked at her friend. "Are you sure it is not too slippery for my hooves?" she asked.

"It is safe for you, Deer," answered Jaguarundi, barely able to keep from laughing.

Deer climbed onto the fallen mahogany tree and carefully began to walk over the stream. She had gone about halfway across when her hooves slipped on the damp wood. She tried to run to the other side, but the tree was very wet, and she fell into the stream. Deer stood up. Water dripped from her chin. Water dripped from her tail. Water dripped from every part of Deer. Jaguarundi rolled on the grassy bank and laughed at his friend.

"Oh, no," cried Deer, "the loaf of bread that I baked for Jaguar and his bride is ruined."

"We still have the pot of juice," said Jaguarundi. "Come, let us be going."

Deer was angry, but as usual, she forgave her friend and continued to travel with him to the wedding feast. As they walked, they passed beneath a guava tree. Jaguarundi looked up into the tree and chuckled.

"Stop, Deer," said Jaguarundi. "I'll climb this guava tree and shake loose some of the delicious fruit. You can gather up as many as you like to take to Jaguar instead of the ruined bread."

"How kind of you to help me find a gift," said Deer as she stood beneath the tree waiting to catch the fruit.

Jaguarundi shook the tree with all his might. The fruit fell down onto Deer. Many of the guavas were soft and too ripe. Jaguarundi laughed as Deer was pelted with

rotten fruit and covered with its sticky juice.

He asked, "Did you get enough guavas?"

Deer was very angry. She had groomed herself carefully for this feast and now her fur was matted and soiled. Deer didn't answer Jaguarundi, but walked quietly beside him to the wedding.

After they arrived, while Deer was in Anteater's hut grooming her fur coat, Jaguarundi told the other guests what had happened on the way to the celebration. Jaguarundi laughed at his jokes, but the other animals didn't laugh. Instead, when Jaguarundi was over on the other side of the clearing beneath a rosewood tree pulling Marmoset's long fluffy tail, they decided to teach the joker a lesson.

The wedding was to be held in late afternoon, because during the hottest part of the day, the animals planned to take a nap. Soon all the forest creatures settled down for their nap, but only Jaguarundi and Deer fell asleep. Instead of sleeping, Frog hopped over to Jaguarundi and smeared some of the stew prepared for the feast upon Jaguarundi's mouth. Then Anaconda, a very,

very large snake, hid the stew pot and put an empty pot in its place on the table. Later, Tapir, a shy animal who had hooves that didn't match, woke up the wedding guests.

Jaguarundi was busy teasing Tapir, because he has three toes on his back feet and four toes on his front feet, when Turtle poked him. Turtle frowned at the brown cat and asked," Jaguarundi, what is that on your mouth? Surely it isn't the stew for today's feast?"

Jaguarundi licked his lips. He tasted stew. "I don't know how I got this stew on my mouth. I was napping just like the rest of you."

Jaguar roared. He pointed at the empty pot. Then Jaguar's bride began to cry and all the animals except Deer shook their paws and hooves at Jaguarundi. They told him to leave the celebration at once.

"But I didn't eat the stew," protested Jaguarundi. "Doesn't anyone believe me?"

Slowly, the little forest Deer walked over to her friend. She looked at the angry animals and remembered all the nasty jokes Jaguarundi had played on her.

"Friends," said Deer, "Jaguarundi doesn't know when to stop playing jokes. Still, I do not believe he ate the stew. If he must leave the wedding feast, then I will leave also."

"You must not leave the feast because of me," said Jaguarundi. "Stay and enjoy yourself, Deer. It is enough that you believed me. I'm sorry I played those tricks on you. You are a good friend."

Just as Jaguarundi was ready to walk away, Jaguar finally said that the brown jungle cat could stay at the celebration as long as he promised to stop playing jokes on Deer and the rest of the forest animals.

"Remember, Jaguarundi," said Jaguar, "you must treat your friends the way you would like to be treated." As Jaguar spoke, Tapir pulled a heavy pot from its hiding place behind a stump. Jaguarundi lifted the lid and peered inside the pot. Jaguar continued, "The stew is safe. We played a joke on you. Was it funny?"

"No," said Jaguarundi, "it wasn't funny for me." The small, brown cat scratched his head and thought for a moment. Then he smiled and said, "I think I'd better play fewer jokes on my friends."

The animals cheered. Jaguarundi, Deer, Jaguar and

his bride, and all their friends had a wonderful wedding feast. They had so much fun, that the celebration did not end until Moon and his best friend Bat were in the sky. But that is another tale!"

All the children looked at Pablo and Carlos. Pablo and Carlos looked at each other and then at Uncle Berto. "We are sorry," they said. "We didn't mean to be so much trouble. We want to play soccer with our friends."

"What about all the jokes?" asked Rosa.

"We will play fewer jokes on our friends," answered the twins.

The children cheered. They stood up and ran out into the yard to play soccer again. Before she ran off of the porch, Rosa gave her Uncle a hug.

Uncle Berto winked his eye and said, "Go have fun with your friends, little deer."

Rosa laughed and joined Carlos, Pablo, Mitsue, David, Bina, Franklin, Tia, Jasmine, Kristin, and the rest of the children in a game of soccer. Meanwhile, Uncle Berto called all the parents of the children on the phone. He invited them to come over to the Sanchez family's house for a pitch-in dinner to celebrate friendship.

Uncle Berto's Pitch-In
☼ Dinner Recipes ☼

Blended Fruit Drink
(Serves 4)

3 ripe bananas, peeled
6 strawberries, leaves removed
4 cups orange juice

1) Put all ingredients in a blender cup and blend for 2 minutes.*
2) Chill in the refrigerator. Serve cold.

Variations: Use different fruit juices and other fruits such as peaches and apples. Remember to remove firm peels and seeds from fruits.

*Ask an adult to help you use a blender. Remember to unplug the blender when you are finished blending the fruits. ☺

Eggless Banana Pancakes
(Serves 2)

1/2 cup rolled oats
1/2 cup flour
1/2 cup cornmeal (white or yellow)
1 tablespoon baking powder
1-1/2 cups water
2 to 3 bananas, peeled and sliced* or mashed
2 teaspoons oil

1) Mix all the ingredients except oil, together in a bowl.
2) Pour about 1/4 cup of the batter into oiled, preheated frying pan.** (The batter will make 4 pancakes).
3) Fry over low heat on one side until lightly browned, then flip over pancake and fry on the other side until done.

Variations: Add raisins, blueberries, or chopped apples* to batter.

*Ask an adult to be in the kitchen when you use a knife to slice the bananas (or chop the apples). ☺
**Ask an adult to help with the stove. Remember to use pot holders or mitts when picking up a hot frying pan. ☺

Little Deer's Fruit Kabobs

(Serves 8)

2 apples, cored and chopped into bite-size pieces*
2 pears, cored and chopped into bite-size pieces*
2 bananas, peeled and sliced into bite-size pieces*
1/4 pineapple, peeled and cored, then chopped
      into bite-size pieces*
1 cup seedless grapes or fresh strawberries

1) Place the chopped fruits on 8 skewers. Make sure to alternate the different fruits.
2) Serve.

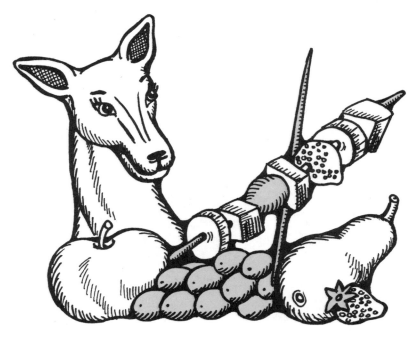

Ask an adult to be in the kitchen when you use a knife to core, peel, or chop the fruits. ☺

Uncle Berto's Bean Tacos

(Serves 6)

1 large onion, peeled and chopped*
2 cloves of garlic, peeled and finely chopped*
1 tablespoon oil
19-ounce can kidney beans, drained (or 2 cups
    of cooked kidney beans), mashed
1 cup frozen or fresh corn kernels
1/4 teaspoon crushed oregano
Salt and pepper to taste
Taco shells
Shredded lettuce and chopped tomatoes*

1) Sauté onion and garlic in oil.
2) Add mashed beans and corn. Add spices and mix well.
3) Heat 5 - 10 minutes over medium heat, stirring occasionally.** Add water if necessary to prevent sticking.
4) Serve in heated taco shells with shredded lettuce and chopped tomatoes.

*Ask an adult to be in the kitchen when you use a knife to chop the vegetables. ☺
**Ask an adult to help with the stove. Remember to use pot holders or mitts when picking up hot pots. ☺

Mexican Succotash
(Serves 6)

1/2 cup onions, peeled and chopped*
2 tablespoons oil
1 pound zucchini, sliced*
1 green pepper - seeds removed, cored and
    chopped*
1/4 cup pimientos, finely chopped*
2 large tomatoes, chopped*
1-1/2 cups corn (frozen, fresh, or canned)
Salt and pepper, to taste

1) Sauté chopped onions over medium heat in oil.**
2) Add remaining ingredients and simmer over low heat
until vegetables are tender. Add a little water if necessary
to prevent sticking.
3) Serve.

*Ask an adult to be in the kitchen when you use a knife to slice
and chop the vegetables. ☺
**Ask an adult to help with the stove. Remember to use pot
holders or mitts when picking up hot pots. ☺

Rosa's Favorite Guacamole

(Serves 4)

1 large or 2 small ripe avocados
1 small ripe tomato, chopped finely*
Garlic powder and cayenne pepper to taste**

1) Cut avocados in half.* Remove pits and spoon out the flesh. Mash avocados in a bowl.
2) Add chopped tomato and seasonings. Mix well.
3) Serve on tacos, with chips, or as a dip with raw vegetables.

*Ask an adult to be in the kitchen when you use a knife to cut the avocados in half and chop the tomato. ☺
**If cayenne pepper gets on your hands, wash it off immediately. Cayenne pepper could sting if it gets in your eyes or in a cut. ☺

Refried Beans

(Serves 8)

3 cups cooked pinto or kidney beans (canned or
     pre-cooked)
1 large onion, peeled and chopped*
2 tablespoons oil
9 ounces tomato paste
3 to 4 tablespoons chili powder

1) Drain and mash canned or pre-cooked beans in bowl.
2) Sauté chopped onion in oil.**
3) Add tomato paste, chili powder, and mashed beans.
Cook over medium heat until beans are heated through.
4) Serve on chips or in taco shells with shredded lettuce,
chopped tomatoes*, and hot sauce.

*Ask an adult to be in the kitchen when you use a knife to chop the
onion and tomatoes. ☺
**Ask an adult to help with the stove. Remember to use pot
holders or mitts when picking up hot pots. ☺

Jaguar's Wedding Stew

(Serves 4)

2 cups water
1/2 cup corn kernels (fresh, frozen, or canned)
1/2 cup lima beans (fresh, frozen, or canned)
1/2 cup potatoes (pre-cooked or canned),
   chopped*
1/2 cup stewed tomatoes
1 onion, peeled and chopped*
1 teaspoon crushed oregano
1/4 cup fresh parsley, chopped*
Salt and pepper to taste

1) Mix all the ingredients in a large pot.
2) Cook over low heat until hot (about 10 to 15 minutes).**
3) Serve alone or over rice.

Ask an adult to be in the kitchen when you use a knife to chop the potatoes, onion, and parsley. ☺
**Ask an adult to help with the stove. Remember to use pot holders or mitts when picking up hot pots.* ☺

Jaguarundi's Tofu Chili

(Serves 8)

1 pound tofu, chopped into small cubes*
2 tablespoons oil
2 onions, peeled and chopped*
3 green peppers - seeds removed, cored and
      chopped*
28-ounce can crushed tomatoes
15-ounce can black-eyed peas, drained
15-ounce can white beans, drained
2 jalapeno peppers, finely chopped*
Garlic and chili powder to taste

1) Sauté tofu in oil over medium heat for 10 minutes.**
2) Add chopped onions and green peppers, and stir-fry 5 minutes longer.
3) Lower heat. Add tomatoes, peas, beans, jalapeno peppers, and spices to the pan. Simmer over low heat for 12 minutes. You can add some tomato paste if sauce is too thin. You can also freeze the chili to serve later.

Ask an adult to be in the kitchen when you use a knife to chop the onions and peppers. ☺
**Ask an adult to help with the stove. Remember to use pot holders or mitts when picking up hot pans.* ☺

Frozen Banana Treat

(Serves 4)

3 to 4 very ripe bananas, peeled
1/2 cup cocoa
2 tablespoons water

1) Place all ingredients in a blender and blend 3 minutes.*
2) Pour into a pan or plastic container. Freeze, then serve.

*Ask an adult to be in the kitchen when using a blender.
Remember to unplug the blender after you are finished blending
the banana mixture. ☺

The Snow Queen's Unicorn

Many of the children who lived on Park Street and Oak Avenue were in Mr. Weaver's fifth grade class or in Miss Moon's fourth grade class at Wood Park Elementary School. Each year before the winter break, Mr. Weaver and Miss Moon helped the students in their classes plan a Winter Party. Each child was to bring in a special food that their family enjoyed. The classrooms were decorated with pictures and favors the students had made. All the parents and other family members who could come were asked to attend the Winter Party.

The neighborhood children were each trying to pick a food to take to the party. Each child was also trying to find a special family custom or story to tell the class about on the day of the party.

Kristin's mother was busy making a straw wreath for their front door when Kristin came into the kitchen. "Mom," said Kristin, "do you think it will snow soon?"

"I'm not sure, Kristin," said Mrs. Nisbeth, "but I do know the Snow Queen's unicorn has been here."

"Don't be silly," said Kristin. "There is no such thing."

"Of course there is. Just look at the windows. See the ice on the outside that is shaped like plants. The Snow Queen's unicorn draws those designs with his icy horn at night while we sleep," explained Kristin's mother.

"I'm in the fourth grade now. I don't believe in fairy tales anymore," said Kristin with a frown.

"I am thirty," said Mrs. Nisbeth with a smile. "I still believe in the Snow Queen and her unicorn. It is good to keep a little magic in your life, even when you get older."

Just then, someone knocked on the door. It was Tia Harris and Jasmine Abdul. Kristin asked her mother if her friends could come in.

"Sure," answered Mrs. Nisbeth. "Maybe they would like to hear about the Snow Queen and her unicorn."

Kristin rolled her eyes. "Come on in," she said. "My mom was trying to tell me one of her fairy tales again. Do you want to hear the story or do you want to go into the living room and play a game?"

Tia looked at Jasmine. Jasmine looked at Tia. They shrugged their shoulders. "We could listen to the story for a few minutes," said Jasmine.

Kristin's mother nodded. "While I'm telling the story, you three may take the shells off of these nuts." Mrs. Nisbeth put a bowl of nuts in front of the girls. She also gave Kristin, Tia, and Jasmine each a glass of juice to drink.

"Long ago," began Kristin's mother, "in the land to the north, there lived a queen. She was not an ordinary queen and her country was not an ordinary place, because almost everything in this land was made of ice and snow. It is for that reason, that she became known as the Snow Queen. Her castle was carved out of an ice mountain. Her furniture was made of cold gray stone and ice. Her castle was guarded by white wolves and polar bears and no one

ever came to visit.

The Snow Queen was lonely; so one day she decided to visit the warmer lands of her neighbors. She wrapped some food in packets and put it in a sack. She put on her skis, picked up her sack, and began the long trip to the warmer lands. The Snow Queen traveled for five days, but everywhere she went, it snowed. She could see green valleys below her, but as soon as she skied down the mountain sides to the valleys, it would start to snow. Before long, the valleys would be white and all the people would be locked tight in their warm homes.

The Snow Queen traveled for five more days. The same thing happened. It seemed that everywhere she went, she brought cold and snow. Now the Snow Queen was not only cold and lonely, she was tired. "What am I to do?" she cried. "Is there no one to keep me company? Is there no one who wants to live in a beautiful ice castle?"

"Who is that fussing outside my cave?" called a deep voice. The Snow Queen was so surprised to hear someone answer her, she couldn't talk. "Speak up," shouted the voice, "we trolls like nice loud voices."

"The Snow Queen," she said. "I'm the Snow Queen."

A big, strong troll climbed out of a cave right beside the Snow Queen. His arms were so long that his fingers touched the ground. His nose was as big and bumpy as a sweet potato. His hair looked like tangled vines and his feet were very large. "The Snow Queen," repeated the troll. "What sort of name is that? What is your real name?"

The Snow Queen thought for a moment. It had been a long time since someone had wanted to know her real name. "Aurora," she answered, "I was named after the colored lights in the northern sky."

"Well," said the troll, "what seems to be the problem?"

"I'm lonely in my ice palace. White wolves and polar bears are not very friendly. And it seems that everywhere I go, I bring so much snow and cold with me that people go inside and lock their doors. I am not a welcome guest," said Queen Aurora.

"I like snow," said the troll. "Most trolls like snow. In fact, we never seem to get enough snow. I will make a deal with you, Aurora. If you promise to visit our green land each year for a few months, I'll find you a friend to live in your ice castle."

"Agreed," said Aurora. "But where will you find someone who wants to live in a world of snow and ice?"

"In my cave," laughed the troll. "Come on out, my friend. Aurora has made our land white; so you are safe from the hunters."

Out of the cave stepped a white horse with a silver horn sticking out of the center of his forehead. Standing on

the snow with flakes falling down, the animal was hard to see.

"What are you?" asked the Snow Queen.

"A unicorn," answered the beautiful animal. "I'm one of the last of my kind. Here in this green land, we are easy to see. Hunters from the king's court capture us and try to make us pets, but unicorns must run free, or they die."

"A land of white sounds wonderful to me," the unicorn continued. "I will keep you company and play chess and checkers with you in the evenings. I'll tell you stories of the many lands I have seen. And together, we can come visit my friends, the trolls, every year."

Aurora was so happy, that she hugged the unicorn and kissed him on his forehead beside the horn. The unicorn's horn sparkled an icy silver. After that kiss from the Snow Queen, the unicorn could draw ice pictures with his horn.

And to this day, once a year, the Snow Queen and the unicorn pack their things and visit the trolls in the green lands. The trolls get to enjoy some snow, Queen Aurora and the unicorn get to visit with their friends, and the unicorn gets to draw ice pictures on as many windows as he likes." Kristin's mother finished talking and smiled.

"That was a good story, Mrs. Nisbeth," said Jasmine. "Thank you for telling it to us."

"Thanks," said Tia. "I like the idea of a unicorn painting my windows."

"Well, I don't think I believe in the Snow Queen or her unicorn," said Kristin. "But it was a good story. Come on, let's go into the living room to play a game."

After the girls left the kitchen, Kristin's mother finished her wreath and hung it on the front door. She scooped up the nuts the girls had shelled and put them in a bowl to use later.

The day of the Winter Party finally came. All the children brought their favorite foods. Many of their family members were able to come to the party. Mr. Weaver and Miss Moon asked if any of the children had brought things

to share.

David stood up. He had drawn a picture of a Chanukah menorah, or nine-branched candlestick. He told why his family celebrated the Festival of Lights and how each night of Chanukah his mother lit one more candle.

Next, Rosa told how the Sanchez family decorated their house with pine and holly in December. Rosa talked about exchanging gifts on Christmas day. Carlos and Pablo raised their hands and said that they also put candles in their windows and hung lights on a pine tree.

Franklin Harris spoke next. Franklin had drawn a picture of a corn plant, some fruit, and a cup. He told the class that these were symbols his family used when they celebrated being African Americans. His sister Tia had painted a picture. Tia's painting was of candles. Her candle holder had room for seven candles. She told the class that the candles were to show the seven important parts of the Kwanza tradition.

Mitsue stood up next. She talked about Chinese New Year. She said, "The Chinese New Year doesn't happen on January 1st, but in late January or early February. There are parades and visits to relatives. Also there are special foods to be eaten. Most of these foods don't contain meat. Because the color red is suppose to bring good luck, red foods and gifts wrapped in red paper are important "

Bina, Jasmine, and many other children talked about their families' special winter celebrations and stories. Even Mr. Harris and Miss Moon talked about their favorite winter celebrations.

Suddenly, Carlos and Pablo began to shout, "It's snowing! It's snowing!" All of the children were excited.

Kristin stood up and spoke, "It is the Snow Queen and her unicorn."

"Tell us more about this Snow Queen, Kristin," said Miss Moon.

"Oh, it's just some dumb old fairy tale," said Carlos.

"No it isn't," said Kristin. "It is a winter tradition in my house. It's a good story to listen to, because everyone needs a little magic in their lives." Kristin looked at her mother and smiled. "But I cannot tell the story as well as my mom, so I'd like her to tell everyone the story of Queen Aurora and her unicorn. Is that okay, Miss Moon?"

Miss Moon nodded. "I think we all could use a bit of magic on a snowy day," she said.

So while the children, their families, and their teachers enjoyed the many wonderful foods; Mrs. Nisbeth told the story of the Snow Queen and her unicorn. Kristin's mother told the tale so well, that all the children behaved themselves, even Carlos and Pablo.

When the Winter Party was over, the children and their families walked home. Some of the children looked for ski tracks and unicorn prints in the snow. Kristin held her mother's hand, laughed, and wondered if there were any trolls in this part of town for the Snow Queen and her unicorn to visit.

❄❄ School Winter ❄❄ ❄ Party Recipes ❄

Unicorn's Golden Chutney
(Serves 6)

1 cup dried figs, chopped*
1 apple, cored and chopped*
1/2 lemon with seeds removed, chopped
        (including peel)*
1/2 cup molasses
1/4 cup vinegar
1 teaspoon ground allspice
1/2 teaspoon ground cinnamon

1) Place ingredients in a pot.
2) Bring to boil over medium heat, then simmer over low
heat for 25 minutes.**
3) Serve hot or cold.

*Ask an adult to be in the kitchen when you use a knife to core the
apples and chop the fruits. ☺
**Ask an adult to help you with the stove. Remember to use pot
holders or mitts when picking up hot pots. ☺

Franklin's Corn Fritters

(Serves 3 to 4)

1/2 cup cornmeal
1/2 cup cooked corn kernels
2/3 cup whole wheat pastry or unbleached
    white flour
1/4 cup cornstarch
2 tablespoons tamari or soy sauce
Dash of pepper
2/3 cup soy milk <u>or</u> water

1) Combine all the ingredients together, mixing well.
2) Form 8 fritters and fry in a lightly oiled pan over medium-high heat until lightly browned.* Turn fritters over and continue cooking until brown on both sides.
3) Serve.

Ask an adult to help with the stove. Remember to use pot holders or mitts when picking up the hot frying pan. ☺

Syrian Wheat Pudding

(Serves 8)

1-1/2 cups bulgur (cracked wheat)
4 cups water
1 cup raisins
1/2 teaspoon caraway seeds
1 tablespoon shelled pistachio nuts
1 tablespoon shelled walnuts, chopped*
1/4 cup maple syrup

1) Place bulgur, water, raisins, and caraway seeds in a covered pot. Cook over medium heat for 30 minutes.** Stir occasionally.
2) Add nuts and syrup. Simmer 5 minutes longer.
3) Serve warm. Cold leftovers are delicious, too!

*Ask an adult to be in the kitchen when you use a knife to chop the nuts. ☺
**Ask an adult to help you with the stove. Remember to use pot holders or mitts when picking up hot pots. ☺

Mitsue's Chinese Stir-Fried Vegetables and Pineapple

(Serves 4)

1 tablespoon oil
1 cup water
3 carrots, chopped*
1 zucchini, chopped*
6 ounces snowpeas (optional)
1/2 pound mushrooms, chopped*
2 onions, peeled and sliced*
2 large tomatoes, chopped*
1/2 pound mung bean sprouts
10-ounce can crushed pineapple, drained
2 tablespoons soy sauce or tamari

1) Stir-fry all the ingredients together over medium-high heat until carrots are tender, yet crisp.**
2) Serve hot with rice.

Variation: Add baby corn and water chestnuts and stir-fry with the other vegetables.

*Ask an adult to be in the kitchen when you use a knife to chop and slice the vegetables. ☺
**Ask an adult to help with the stove. Remember to use pot holders or mitts when picking up hot pans. ☺

Kristin's Favorite Vegetable Soup

(Serves 6)

3 carrots, peeled and finely chopped*
3 stalks celery, finely chopped*
1 small zucchini, finely chopped*
1 onion, peeled and finely chopped*
2 teaspoons oil
8 cups water
14-1/2 ounce can whole peeled tomatoes,
    chopped* <u>or</u> use a can of crushed
    tomatoes
1 cup fresh or frozen peas or corn kernels
1/4 cup fresh parsley, finely chopped*
Salt and pepper to taste

1) Sauté carrots, celery, zucchini, and onion in oil in a large pot over medium-high heat for 5 minutes.** Add water and bring to a boil. Reduce heat, cover pot, and simmer for 25 minutes.
2) Add remaining ingredients and simmer 20 minutes longer. Serve hot.

*Ask an adult to be in the kitchen when you use a knife to chop the vegetables. ☺
**Ask an adult to help with the stove. Be careful when removing the lid from a hot pot. Remember to use pot holders or mitts when picking up hot lids or pots. ☺

Troll's Tasty Hot Apple Cider

(Serves 8)

1/2 gallon apple cider
1 lemon, seeds removed, sliced thinly*
1 or 2 teaspoons ground cinnamon
1/4 teaspoon ground nutmeg

1) Heat ingredients in a large pot over medium heat.**
Stir occasionally, until heated through.
2) Serve warm.

*Ask an adult to be in the kitchen when you use a knife to slice the lemon. ☺

**Ask an adult to help you with the stove. Remember to use pot holders or mitts when picking up the hot pot. ☺

Hummus

(Serves 8)

4 cups pre-cooked or canned (two 19-ounce cans)
  garbanzo beans (chickpeas), drained
1/2 cup water
3 tablespoons tahini (sesame butter)
2 tablespoons lemon juice
1 teaspoon sesame oil
1 teaspoon garlic powder
1 teaspoon cumin
Salt and pepper to taste

1) Place all ingredients in a blender. Blend until creamy.*
2) Chill before serving with pita bread.

*Ask an adult to be in the kitchen when you use a blender. Make
sure to unplug the blender when you are finished blending the
hummus.* ☺

Jasmine's Favorite Pita Bread

(Serves 8)

1 tablespoon active dry yeast
1-1/2 cups warm water
3 cups unbleached white flour
1-1/2 cups whole wheat pastry flour
1-1/2 teaspoons salt

1) Dissolve yeast in water and add to dry ingredients in a large bowl.
2) Mix well and knead for 5 minutes. Cover bowl and let dough rise in a warm place for 3 hours.
3) Preheat over to 375 degrees Fahrenheit.*
4) Divide dough into 8 balls. Roll each ball out into a 6-inch wide by 1/2-inch thick circle.
5) Place flattened dough onto an ungreased baking sheet.
6) Bake at 375 degrees Fahrenheit for 10 minutes until pita bread is light brown.*
7) Serve warm and store leftovers in a plastic bag.

Ask an adult to help with the oven. Remember to use pot holders or mitts when picking up hot baking sheets. ☺

Apple Raisin Spice Muffins

(Makes 18 Muffins)

1 cup unbleached white flour
2 cups whole wheat flour
1 teaspoon baking powder
1/2 teaspoon baking soda
1 teaspoon ground cinnamon
1/4 teaspoon ground nutmeg
1/2 teaspoon ground allspice
1 cup water
1/3 cup maple syrup or molasses
2 apples, cored and chopped finely*
1/2 cup raisins

1) Preheat oven to 400 degrees Fahrenheit.**
2) Mix all of the ingredients together in a large bowl.
3) Pour batter into lightly oiled muffin tins. Bake for 20 minutes at 400 degrees Fahrenheit.**
4) Let muffins cool before removing from tins.

Variation: Add 1/2 cup chopped walnuts to batter before baking. *

Ask an adult to be in the kitchen when you use a knife to core and chop the apples and chop the walnuts. ☺
***Ask an adult to help with the oven. Remember to use pot holders or mitts when picking up hot muffin tins.* ☺

Carlos and Pablo's Spanish Rice

(Serves 4)

1 tablespoon oil
1 onion, peeled and chopped finely*
1 green pepper - seeds removed, cored and
    chopped finely*
1-1/2 cups rice, precooked (instant or leftover rice)
3 tomatoes, cubed*
1 small can tomato sauce
Pepper, cumin, and chili powder to taste

1) In a large nonstick skillet, heat oil over medium heat.** Sauté onion and green pepper until onion is golden.
2) Add cooked rice, tomatoes, tomato sauce, and seasoning. Cook 10 more minutes.** Serve.

*Ask an adult to be in the kitchen when you use a knife to chop and cube the vegetables. ☺
**Ask an adult to help with the stove. Remember to use pot holders or mitts when picking up hot skillets. ☺

Potato Pancakes

(Serves 6)

3 cups potatoes - cooked and mashed, or
   raw and grated*
1 onion, peeled and chopped*
Pepper and salt to taste
Handful of fresh parsley, finely chopped* (optional)
2 tablespoons oil

1) Mix onion and seasonings with potatoes. Form 6 pancakes from mixture.
2) Heat oil in pan over medium heat.** Fry pancakes until lightly browned. Turn over pancakes and fry on other side until golden brown.

Ask an adult to be in the kitchen when you use a knife to chop onion and a grater to grate potato. ☺
**Ask an adult to help with the stove. Remember to use pot holders or mitts when picking up hot pans. ☺*

✤For More Information ✤

To learn more about myths, folklore, and fairy tales, check your local library. The library is a good place to find other children's cookbooks and books about vegetarian cooking, too. Other places to learn more about vegetarian cooking are the *Vegetarian Resource Group* publications listed in the back of this book. For more information about vegetarianism, you can read the following publications and vegetarian magazines.

Publications:

Center for Science in the Public Interest. Creative Food Experiences for Children, 1875 Connecticut Avenue, N.W., Suite 300, Washington, DC 20009-5728. (202) 332-9110.

Hurwitz, Johanna. Much Ado About Aldo, Morrow Junior Books, 1978.

Klaper, Michael, M.D. Pregnancy, Children, and the Vegan Diet, Gentle World, Inc., 1987.

Mangels, Reed, Ph.D., R.D. The Vegan Diet During Pregnancy, Lactation, and Childhood, The Vegetarian Resource Group, 16 pages, $3.00.

Wasserman, Debra & Stahler, Charles. I Love Animals and Broccoli, Children's Activity Book, The Vegetarian Resource Group, 1985, 48 pages, $5.00

Vegetarian Magazines:

Vegetarian Gourmet, P. O. Box 7641, Riverton, NJ 08077.
Vegetarian Journal, P. O. Box 1463, Baltimore, MD 21203.
Vegetarian Times, P. O. Box 446, Mount Morris, IL 61054.
Veggie Life, P. O. Box 57159, Boulder, CO 80323.

Other Books Available ✦ From The Vegetarian ✦ ✦✦✦ Resource Group ✦✦✦

If you wish to purchase one or more of the following VRG titles, please send a check or money order made payable to *The Vegetarian Resource Group* (Maryland residents must add 5% sales tax) and mail it with your order to: *The Vegetarian Resource Group, P. O. Box 1463, Baltimore, MD 21203.* Make sure you include your shipping address. Or call (410) 366-VEGE to order with Mastercard or Visa credit card. Price given includes postage in the United States. Outside the USA, please pay in US funds by credit card or money order and add $2.00 per book for postage.

SIMPLE, LOWFAT & VEGETARIAN

Unbelievably <u>Easy Ways</u> to <u>Reduce the Fat in Your Meals!</u> by Suzanne Havala, M.S., R.D. Recipes by Mary Clifford, R.D. Foreword by Dean Ornish, M.D.

An easy-to-use guidebook to lowfat eating. How to enjoy Chinese, Mexican, Italian, Indian, and fast food. Chapters on bag lunches, amusement parks, pizza, movies, cafeterias, salad bars, planes, trains, cruise ships,and more. For each type of eating, *Menu Magic* gives you a few simple changes to reduce the fat in a typical meal. Additional help with *Good Choices, Fat Content of Selected Items,* and *Helpful Hints.* Includes shopping lists, recipes, 30 days of quick meals, over 100 lowfat brands found in natural foods stores, weight loss chapters, ideas for vegans, and help in revising your own recipes.

TRADE PAPERBACK, $14.95

MEATLESS MEALS FOR WORKING PEOPLE
Quick and Easy Vegetarian Recipes
by Debra Wasserman & Charles Stahler

Vegetarian cooking can be simple or complicated. *The Vegetarian Resource Group* recommends using whole grains and fresh vegetables whenever possible. However, for the busy working person, this isn't always possible. Meatless Meals For Working People contains over 100 delicious, fast, and easy recipes, plus ideas which teach you how to be a vegetarian within your hectic schedule by using common, convenient, vegetarian foods. This handy guide also contains a spice chart, party ideas, information on fast food chains, and much more.

TRADE PAPERBACK, $6

THE LOWFAT JEWISH VEGETARIAN COOKBOOK
HEALTHY TRADITIONS FROM AROUND THE WORLD
by Debra Wasserman

Serves up over 150 delicious, healthy dishes, including 33 suitable for Passover. Feast on Romanian Apricot Dumplings, Czechoslovakian Noodles with Poppy Seeds, or Polish Apple Blintzes, Potato Knishes, Indian Curry, Greek Pastry, and Spinach Pies. Celebrate with Eggless Challah, Hamentashen for Purim, Passover Vegetable Kishke, Chanukah Latkes, Russian Charoset, Mock Chopped "Liver," Eggless Matzoh Balls, and much more. Each recipe contains a nutritional analysis. Also includes Rosh Hashanah dinner suggestions, a glossary of foods used in Jewish vegetarian cooking, and lists of the top ten recipes for calcium and iron.

TRADE PAPERBACK, $15

NO CHOLESTEROL PASSOVER RECIPES - 100 VEGETARIAN RECIPES
by Debra Wasserman & Charles Stahler

For many, low-calorie Passover recipes are a challenge. Here is a wonderful collection of Passover dishes that are non-dairy, eggless, no-cholesterol, and vegetarian. It includes recipes for eggless blintzes, dairyless carrot cream soup, festive macaroons, apple latkes, sweet and sour cabbage, knishes, broccoli with almond sauce, mock "chopped liver," no oil lemon dressing, eggless matzo meal pancakes, and much more.

PAPERBACK, $9

VEGETARIAN QUANTITY RECIPES
From The Vegetarian Resource Group

Here is a helpful kit for people who must cook for large groups and institutional settings. It contains 28 vegetarian recipes, including main dishes, burgers, sandwich spreads, side dishes, soups, salads, desserts, and breakfast foods. Each recipe provides a serving for 25 and 50 people, and a nutritional analysis. The kit also contains a listing of companies offering vegetarian food items in institutional sizes and "Tips For Introducing Vegetarian Food Into Institutions."

PACKET, $15

VEGETARIAN JOURNAL REPORTS
Edited by Debra Wasserman & Charles Stahler

This 112-page book consists of the best articles from previous *Vegetarian Journals*. Included are a 28-Day Meal Plan, a Vegetarian Weight Loss Guide, Tips for Changing Your Diet, a Vegetarian Guide for Athletes, Information for Diabetic Diets, plus Indian Recipes, Eggless Dishes, and many more vegetarian resources.

PAPERBACK, $12

SIMPLY VEGAN

QUICK VEGETARIAN MEALS by Debra Wasserman, Nutrition Section by Reed Mangels, Ph.D., R.D.

An easy-to-use vegetarian guide that contains over 160 kitchen-tested vegan recipes (no meat, fish, fowl, dairy, or eggs.) Each recipe is accompanied by a nutritional analysis. Reed Mangels, Ph.D., R.D., has included an extensive vegan nutrition section on topics such as Protein, Fat, Calcium, Iron, Vitamin B12, Pregnancy and the Vegan Diet, Feeding Vegan Children, and Calories, Weight Gain, and Weight Loss. A Nutritional Glossary is provided, along with sample menus, meal plans, and a list of the top recipes for iron, calcium, and Vitamin C. Also featured are food definitions and origins, and a comprehensive list of mail-order companies that specialize in selling vegan food, natural clothing, cruelty-free cosmetics, and ecologically-safe household products.

TRADE PAPERBACK, $12

THE VEGETARIAN GAME

This computer software educational game contains 750 questions. Learn while having fun. Categories include health/nutrition, how food choices affect the environment, animals and ethical choices, vegetarian foods, famous vegetarians, and potluck. Three age levels: 5 - 9; 10 or older/adults new to vegetarianism; and individuals with advanced knowledge of vegetarianism or anyone looking for a challenge. IBM PC-compatible, with CGA or better or Hercules graphics MS DOS 2.0 or higher.

SOFTWARE, $19.95
(When ordering, indicate 3.5" or 5.25" disk.)

VEGETARIAN JOURNAL'S GUIDE TO NATURAL FOODS RESTAURANTS IN THE U.S. AND CANADA

OVER 2,000 LISTINGS OF RESTAURANTS & VACATION SPOTS

For the health-conscious traveler, this is the perfect traveling companion to insure a great meal -- or the ideal lodgings -- when away from home. And for those who are looking for a nearby place to eat, this unique guide offers a host of new and interesting possibilities. As people have become more health-conscious, there has been a delightful proliferation of restaurants designed to meet the growing demand for healthier meals. To help locate these places, there is now a single source for information on over 2,000 restaurants, vacation resorts, and more.

The Vegetarian Journal's Guide to Natural Foods Restaurants (Avery Publishing Group, Inc.) is a helpful guide listing eateries state by state and province by province. Each entry not only describes the house specialties, varieties of cuisine, and special dietary menus, but also includes information on ambiance, attire, and reservations. It even tells you whether or not you can pay by credit card. And there's more. Included in this guide are listings of vegetarian inns, spas, camps, tours, travel agencies, and vacation spots.

PAPERBACK, $13

VEGETARIAN JOURNAL'S FOOD SERVICE UPDATE NEWSLETTER

This three-times-a-year newsletter is for food service personnel and others working for healthier food in schools, restaurants, hospitals, and other institutions. Vegetarian Journal's Food Service Update Newsletter offers advice, shares recipes, and spotlights leaders in the industry who are providing the healthy options consumers are seeking.

SAMPLE NEWSLETTER, $3

SUBSCRIBE TO
VEGETARIAN JOURNAL

The practical magazine for those interested in health, ecology, and ethics.

Each issue features:
- ◆ Nutrition Hotline ---answers your questions about vegetarian diets.
- ◆ Low-fat Vegetarian Recipes -- quick and easy dishes, international cuisine, and gourmet meals.
- ◆ Natural Food Product Reviews
- ◆ Scientific Updates -- a look at recent scientific papers relating to vegetarianism.
- ◆ Vegetarian Action -- projects by individuals and groups.

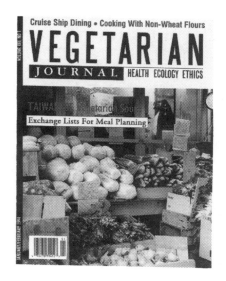

VEGETARIAN Journal ISSN 0885-7636 is published bi-monthly by the independent Vegetarian Resource Group.

To receive a one-year subscription, send a check for $20 to *The Vegetarian Resource Group, P. O. Box 1463, Baltimore, MD 21203.* Canadian and Mexican subscriptions are $30 per year and other foreign country subscriptions are $40 per year. All non-USA subscriptions must be paid in U.S. funds by postal money order or Mastercard/Visa credit card.

Name: _____

Address: _____

_____ Zip: _____

What is The Vegetarian ✦✦ Resource Group? ✦✦

Our health professionals, activists, and educators work with businesses and individuals to bring about healthy changes in your school, workplace, and community. Registered dietitians and physicians aid in the development of practical, nutrition-related publications and answer member or media questions about the vegetarian diet.

Vegetarian Journal **is one of the benefits members enjoy.** Readers receive practical tips for vegetarian meal planning, articles on vegetarian nutrition, recipes, natural food product reviews, and an opportunity to share ideas with others. All nutrition articles are reviewed by a registered dietitian or medical doctor.

The Vegetarian Resource Group is a non-profit organization. Financial support comes primarily from memberships, contributions, and book sales. **Membership includes the bimonthly *Vegetarian Journal*. To join, send $20 to The Vegetarian Resource Group, P.O. Box 1463, Baltimore, MD 21203.**

✛✛✛✛✛ Index ✛✛✛✛✛

Additional Copies of

Leprechaun Cake
and Other Tales,
A Vegetarian Story-Cookbook

may be purchased by sending $10.00
(Maryland Residents add 5% sales tax) to:

The Vegetarian Resource Group
P.O. Box 1463, Baltimore, MD 21203
Inquire about orders in quantity

To join
The Vegetarian Resource Group
and Receive the Bimonthly

Vegetarian Journal

for One Year
Send $20.00 to the Above Address